T0199073

Jango the Little Dragon

The Wondrous Adventures of Little Dragon

Doris Soli

AuthorHouse™ UK
1663 Liberty Drive
Bloomington, IN 47403 USA
www.authorhouse.co.uk
UK TFN: 0800 0148641 (Toll Free inside the UK)
UK Local: 02036 956322 (+44 20 3695 6322 from outside the UK)

Because of the dynamic nature of the Internet, any web addresses or links contained in this
book may have changed since publication and may no longer be valid. The views expressed
in this work are solely those of the author and do not necessarily reflect the views of
the publisher, and the publisher hereby disclaims any responsibility for them.

Any people depicted in stock imagery provided by Getty Images are models,
and such images are being used for illustrative purposes only.
Certain stock imagery © Getty Images.

This book is printed on acid-free paper.

ISBN: 978-1-7283-5462-0 (sc)
978-1-7283-5461-3 (e)

Library of Congress Control Number: 2020911894

Print information available on the last page.

Published by AuthorHouse 07/02/2020

authorHOUSE®

Once upon a time, a very long time ago in the wilderness of time, in ancient times of old, in a beautiful tropical African plain, and in all the ancient lands far and wide, lived friendly animals of all kinds. In this faraway wilderness of land was the Kingdom of Tall Tales.

In this Kingdom lived the charming natured Tiger, Zebra who was quiet and thoughtful, Giraffe who stretched up so high and not forgetting Elephant with wide eyes and flappy ears. The richness and glow of the Sun gave each day a pleasant and beautiful day in this kingdom. All these various animals lived with friendship, strength, courage, wisdom and patience.

Story telling was a special tradition in this big village. At Sunset, all the inhabitants always gathered at a centre point and told stories over a log fire. This centre point was the tallest and huge tree in the village where all the delicious fantasy of stories of imaginations were told and enjoyed. Wonderful stories which had been passed down through countless generations. Lions and Jaguars, Leopards, Tigers and Tortoises, Elephants and Eagles, Hippopotamus, Rhinoceroses and all the different beautiful creatures took turns to tell their stories of undiscovered magical worlds. Lion waving his bushy tail which he admired all day always called for silence so everyone could be heard and gave words of praise and encouragement.

But it was also so long ago that these creatures shared their world with a little Dragon! This dragon was courageous and very kind, but he could not fly. He was the only dragon in the land of Tall Tales who was flightless, but still he had a very special gift. He loved to tell stories, tall stories and short stories, stories of all kinds. Sometimes they were happy, sometimes a little sad, but mostly they were full of adventure and imaginations. As time went by, this flightless dragon knew he was no ordinary dragon. He had that magic dust under his wings and in time, will make him fly one day.

With laughter in his voice, a song in his heart and always with a new story to tell, he entertains his friends day and night.

At sunset the inhabitants would gather together under the tall tree and listen to Jango the Little Dragon, telling his stories around the log fire. They would feast on all kinds of delicious fruits, bananas and breadfruits, pawpaw and pineapples, mangoes and melons and many, many more. Little dragon loved mangoes! He always had loads and loads of mangoes in his mouth until his typical sound of mangoes came out "Jango" instead of mangoes, and he was affectionately called "Jango" the little dragon.

Time went by and a day came when little Jango had a Big Idea – "a very big idea!"

"I can make up so many stories but what about having a real adventure!" he thought to himself.

Yes! he would take some of his friends to explore places beyond their Kingdom to undiscovered magical worlds. An adventure of fantasy, fun and of beautiful excitements.

One evening after an especially entertaining story time, he called on all his friends to announce his Big Idea. As the evening went by, he announced his "Big Idea" adventure.

"Who would like to come with me on a Big Adventure?" he asked.

His friends were so excited that everyone wanted to come with him at once, Lion suggested they all drew straws. The special short straws were drawn by Zebra, Giraffe, Tiger and Elephant. Elephant was known to everyone as "Little Big Ears" because although he was huge now, everyone had known him since he was little! He flapped his ears in complete delight.

Yes! Tomorrow would be a wonderful day! Everyone really loves a good adventure.

They were all so excited that it was hard to sleep that night but the next morning they were ready to leave on their big expedition. Elephant trumpeted "Let's do it!" circling around and around attempting to jump for joy though he couldn't quite manage it.

"Stay calm, stay calm!" yelled Tiger.

"Can we start now?" breathed long-necked Giraffe.

"Surely whinnied Zebra.

"No time like the present!" cried Jango the Little Dragon and trotted forward fearlessly. They then set off into unknown lands. Some of the children of the Kingdom accompanied the party.

Little Dragon, his friends and the little ones walked for miles and miles and some more miles on a lonely track through the grassland and thick forest, they said funny and silly things to each other as they walked along, then out onto dusty plains, weaving their way between enormous towering Baobab trees. Little dragon's trailing wings became covered in dust, and they were all hot and a bit bothered.

Almost immediately, just as they thought they were lost,

"It's all right", said Giraffe from his great height, "I can see a waterhole ahead!"

The five friends and all the little ones raced to the pond under one of the tall trees and bowed their heads for a cooling drink, except for Elephant who sucked the water into his trunk first.

"Handy eh! And no need for a straw!" trumpeted Elephant.

The animals rested by the pool, but what they didn't see were the two huge eyes looking at them from behind a bush. And what they didn't notice was the enormous creature those eyes belonged to!

"Is it just me or is that bush smouldering, I think it's on fire?" observed Zebra.

A very deep roar, louder than any lion, shattered the air.

"Bushes don't generally roar!" suggested Tiger helpfully.

The leaves shook and the ground trembled as a huge animal rose up before them, with shimmering wings spread wide and far, with the tale lashing and a great mouth which breathed a great burst of fire into the air! This was not a little dragon, this was a fully-grown dragon, and it was breathing fire! Fire and more fire!

Little Dragon and friends were rooted to the spot, even Elephant was frightened but in a moment, he acted, spraying water from his trunk and putting out the dragon's fire.

"Oops, will that make it angrier?" whispered Giraffe.

"Perhaps it is hungry," rasped Jango.

But instead they saw a big wet tear fall from the great creature's eye.

"I'm sorry I frightened you, it was only because I was scared too!" gulped the old dragon. "I was on a long flight to see my nephews beyond the mountains. But I got so tired and had to make a landing by this water hole.

"So, you weren't going to eat us after all!" said young Zebra.

"Certainly not!" replied Old Dragon.

"We come from the Kingdom of Tall Tales and we are on a big adventure" announced Jango proudly.

The evening sun was falling, and soon stars began to twinkle above. They gathered firewood near the watering hole, and of course Old Dragon had no trouble in lighting a log fire to keep them all warm. She also unpacked her overnight bag which was full of lovely fruits for them all to share.

"Fritters anyone" she cooed, breathing a gentle flame over the fruits and cooking them instantly.

Little dragon entertained them with more wonderful stories late into the night. Then one by one they fell into a contented sleep, even though Old Dragon did snore quite loudly.

Rays of morning light woke them. They were sorry to see the old Dragon go. Old Dragon insisted on giving each of the friends a soppy kiss goodbye, then with a running jump and a great whooshing of air, took to the skies. "Be good! Bye! Bye! Byeee!" could be heard on the breeze.

Refreshed and happy the adventurers headed out again through the dusty plains towards the woodlands.

"Are we there yet?" laughed Zebra.

"Perhaps there will be a secret passage around the corner!" said Tiger to keep their spirits up.

"If there is a secret passage, I hope I can fit into it!" muttered long-necked Giraffe.

"Me too!" thought Elephant, because he was just too tired to say anything.

"Best foot, paw or hoof forward my friends!" encouraged Jango. Soon they found themselves in a clearing in the forest and as they looked up to the sky, a rainbow appeared from behind a cloud. It shone on them. It was magical to see and as they blinked their eyes open, they found themselves in a garden of rainbows!

A beautiful garden, gardens of waterfalls. Waterfalls that flowed gently, and there was a welcoming and refreshing cooling breeze in the garden. As each gentle drop fell from the waterfalls, one could hear music in the air. Music to dance to. Beautiful water lilies floated in the ponds and lotus flowers surrounded them. The clear water glittered bright with dappled sunlight. Birds, flamingos and graceful swans enjoying the cool waters everywhere.

"What a beautiful place" said Elephant, wide-eyed in disbelief.

"Breathtaking!" whispered Tiger.

The friends glanced at each other, smiled and then jumped into the water for a splash and a swim alongside the graceful swans. As evening approached the lovely swans and flamingos of the rainbow garden arranged parties of fun and cheer to welcome their visitors, and of course Little dragon narrated their stories of their big adventure so far and what they hope to see and find on their journey.

Once more they fell into happy dreams full of the colours of the rainbow. Alas! The magic moment for little dragon had finally arrived. The magic dust under his wings immediately began to work. He could now really fly. Almost immediately little dragon, cheerful as ever, carried his friends over to the next land of adventure. Yes!" in the high blue sky. They could not believe their eyes. They were right high above all the forest tallest trees. What an excitement, an experience never to be forgotten, up in the beautiful blue skies were birds of all various kinds and colours riding on the clouds, singing beautiful melodies, greeted them.

The kids were just so excited they were riding on a blue cloud like a huge blue carpet.

As they went higher and higher, more Songbirds greeted them with beautiful melodies flying gently back and forth between the airborne friends. A warm wind moved them forward again higher and higher.

"I've always dreamed of flying!" shouted little Jango happily. Surrounded by clouds, each animal rode on its own rainbow cloud. This is fantastic shouted Jango again happily. This is pure imagination. "shouted" Tiger.

Sky riding was not something Elephant had expected, and at first, he clung tightly with his trunk to Tiger's tail, but with kind words from Zebra and Giraffe, he gradually let go and floated free on his own. They all glided up and down between the clouds, on this beautiful and wonderful huge blue cloud of a carpet.

Eventually they calmed down enough to enjoy the spectacular view.

Finally, the clouds beneath parted and they saw they were crossing the coastline and travelling out over a limitless blue ocean.

"Awful lot of water down there!" observed Giraffe as she craned her neck downward for a better view, "And we are losing height!"

"We are moving so fast down and we are all going to drown!" shouted the kids.

"Certainly not!" yelled Tiger.

"We are dropping fast; we are going to get very very wet!" said Zebra in a high voice.

"Everyone hold your breath a lot!" suggested Tiger.

Alas, suddenly another high adventure had begun. This time it was a huge pink purplish cloud which gently enveloped them, and they descended into the boundless turquoise ocean. This next land of adventure was so different from what they have ever seen so far or known or heard about before. They were deep, deep, deep down in the blue oceans.

But as they sank down and down into the sea, the pink cloud magically protected them! They floated apart in the Ocean current, each surrounded by their own wispy pink envelope of cloud. They weren't wet at all and they could breathe easily.

They were whisked along in the ocean currents as if on a giant water ride. Soon they were greeted by dolphins as they descended to a tropical reef of beautiful corals. They were now in a new kingdom which they could never have imagined. Multi-coloured fish of different shapes and sizes swam to and from, sea plants waved at them and happy clown octopus with his delightful humour tickled their toes sideways.

They played hide and seek with turtles and had races with sea horses. All the creatures of the reef gathered to meet them, and a happy Octopus entertained everyone by playing empty seashells with all eight legs. He also told very bad jokes.

Octopus and Sea Horses wanted to know all about the Kingdom of Tall Tales and the lands that lay far away from the ocean. Jango the Little Dragon held them spellbound with the story of their journey.

And finally, to end the evening they joined in with a display of synchronised swimming with a troop of specially trained Sea Horses, in appreciation for their newfound friends.

Giraffe said, "I think it's time for us to go, but where and how?"

Tiger asked their friends from the reef how they might get home and an old lobster stepped forward.

He led them in a great procession around a maze of reef canyons until at last they saw the shining entrance to an underwater cave.

The Octopus, Sea Horses and Dolphins chorused their goodbyes and the friends, and the kids stepped towards the light. And would you believe it, as they walked down into the cave, they all started to feel sleepy!

As they woke up, they felt themselves speeding straight upward, floating on a bed of bubbling warm water.

"Whoosh!" yelled the Little Dragon.

He would have said more but in a moment, they were shot into bright daylight. The warm geyser had fired them into a pure white mist, a host of shining points of light. They made a soft landing in banks of powdery snow! Yes!" this was the strangest place of all, whiter than white, glittering snow and snowflakes everywhere.

Tiger's teeth chattered, Zebra shivered, Giraffe shook, rattled and rolled, and Elephant flapped his ears in an attempt to keep his head warm.

"Keep moving and you'll soon warm up!" elephant shouted, and soon they were all sliding in the snow.

"Snowball fight!" shouted the kids spontaneously, rolling the snow into a ball. Snowball play broke out as they went wild throwing snowballs at each other, soon forgot about the cold.

Then they returned to sit beside the warm geyser pool and for the first time looked at the wonderful winter landscape.

Among the snow and snow mountains were varieties of horses and ponies. They were all cute as they were beautiful. Tall and elegant pointed mountains rose all around, capped with snow and reflecting the glittering rays of the sun. The highest mountain of all glowed with blue light and down in the nearby valley, they could see white animals leaving tracks in the snow. Horses and ponies dancing melodiously over the mountain slopes. The kids run down into the valley to greet these new friends. They were so delighted to see these fabulous white Ponies.

"Hello!" said the first Pony, "I am Misty, and here are, Melody and Blue." The kids immediately introduced themselves as "Noble Elephant," "Terrific little Tiger," "Grand Giraffe," the show-off and "Excellent Zebra". Melody and Misty smiled pleasantly. They were all happy to be in such good company. Then the Ponies galloped few paces, and away towards the pointed elegant mountains.

Little Dragon and the adventurous party couldn't believe such amazing mysteries. Everyday had brought a new adventure. They stayed and played in the snow valley for days on end. Time and days went by so quickly.

Finally, after a spellbound story telling session around the warm geyser pools, it was time for goodbyes. All in happy mood they said their goodbyes. Little Dragon was so pleased with his Big Idea - Mission Accomplished.

"How will we get home?" asked Lion.

On the day of departure, Misty and Melody pointed to a magical snow filled path that will take them back home to the Kingdom of Tall Tales.

This was an unforgettable journey for Little Dragon and friends.

With the glow of happiness, smiles, laughter and joy in their hearts, they sang together in clever chorus and hurried along to the beautiful tropical wilderness of time, in all the ancient land of the Kingdom of Tall Tales. The never-ending stories had just begun a new adventure.

THE END

Printed in the United States
By Bookmasters